Galley B

LOS

A.L. BARKER (1918–2002) was a short-story writer and novelist. Born in St Paul's Cray, Kent, and brought up in Beckenham, her first collection of short stories, *The Innocents*, won the Somerset Maugham award in 1947. Though she never achieved as much commercial success as she deserved, Barker boasted a huge array of admirers, including Rebecca West, Evelyn Waugh, A.S. Byatt, Penelope Lively, Jane Gardam, John Sutherland, Adam Mars-Jones, Nina Bawden, and Deborah Moggach. Auberon Waugh said, 'She writes like an angel and I love her.' We do too and we are proud to offer this new edition of 'Lost Journey', perhaps Barker's greatest short story, as one of the launch titles of our new pocket shorts range.

Lost Journey

A.L. Barker

GALLEY BEGGAR PRESS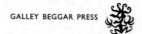

This edition published in 2014
By Galley Beggar Press Limited
37 Dover Street,
Norwich, NR2 3LG

Set in Espinosa Nova by Tetragon, Camden Town
Printed in the UK by CPI Group (UK) Ltd, Croydon, CRO 4YY

A CIP record for this book is available
from the British Library

ISBN 978-1-910296-19-6

Lost Journey

THE first time I saw Gerda Charles it was coming up to the fifth of November and I thought now there's a first-rate guy fawkes. She was in an orange box on wheels, parked in the high street. It so happened that the sun, slanting between Woolworth's and Sainsbury's lit up her face. When she moved, nodded and grinned, I was shocked. I have no great reverence for life, there's too much of it about, but there has to be a line drawn. It ought to be drawn this side of Gerda.

She was like those things that hang out of church gutters – hooked nose, pop eyes and a great long tongue. She was looking up into people's faces and her tongue was darting in and out as if she'd lick them up and swallow them. What bothered me was how she fitted into the orange box which was small and square. So where were her legs?

A girl came out of Sainsbury's with a loaded carrier-bag which she dumped in the box on top of the old woman. A jar of pickled onions fell out, hit the pavement and smashed. Onions rolled under the feet of passers-by. The girl and the old woman laughed. She was pretty, the girl, in a Spanish or Irish way, plump, dark-haired, white-skinned and warm. Her blouse was open at the neck, I could see her throat down to her cleavage, yet it was raw weather and most people were well wrapped up.

I had nothing particular to do, Saturday morning being my free time. I was propping up the wall outside the Grapes, when they opened I would go in and prop up the bar. The girl and the old woman and the broken pickle jar were a bit of fun, that's all they were at that juncture. I wasn't the only one looking at them and smelling vinegar.

The box was fixed into an old pram frame. I watched the girl's very nice breasts bear down on the pram handle to get the cart moving. She bumped it down the kerb, not looking where she was going. A Telecom van screeched to a standstill and the driver yelled at her. She calmly pushed the contraption across the road, the old woman put up two fingers at the Telecom man.

When they reached my side of the street the girl had trouble getting the cart up the kerb. I went to help, it bothered me to see those breasts getting bumped.

'You want to take it easy, this is a busy road.' I lifted the cart by its front axle.

'And?' said the girl.

'You nearly got your mother killed.'

'My mother!' She put her hair back from her face and looked me over. 'Fat chance,' she said calmly. 'Give us a hand up the hill, will you?'

That's how I was caught up with those two. The girl's name was Lalla, if she had another I never knew it. Gerda told me once that she herself was a cousin of Robert Dudley.

'Who's he?' I said, and she said:

'The Earl of Leicester, the Queen's lover.'

'You could be the Duchess of Dillwater,' I said, 'but I never heard of any hanky-panky in that quarter.'

'On my mother's side of the family,' she said. 'Robert and I shared a wet-nurse. And it was Elizabeth Tudor, you bloody fool.'

That came later. As I pushed Gerda up the hill that Saturday I thought here's a turn-up for the book: I wonder what sort of book it was.

They told me they lived at Charlesworth Manor.

'My ancestral home,' said Gerda, with the cackle I now know so well. Charlesworth is a mansion set in acres of ground outside the town and it's been empty for years. They were in fact squatting there.

For reasons best known to myself, and not all connected with Lalla – Gerda herself fascinated and repelled me – I pushed the box-cart up the hill and along the lanes and the length of the overgrown, bramble-bound drive and round to a side door of the house.

'You're blown,' said Gerda. 'A young fellow like you. I'd run rings round you if I had my legs.'

'Well you haven't,' said Lalla. She took the shopping out of the cart and by accident or design the blanket came with it and I saw that all Gerda had was a pair of rusty black trousers sewn into flaps where her legs would have begun.

Those two had broken and entered the house. Boards nailed across the doorframe had been prised off and used to smash the glass panels. After that it would have been easy to reach through and pull back the bolts. I could see Lalla doing it, and Gerda egging her on.

'Suppose you're spotted?' I said.

Lalla shrugged; Gerda said amiably, 'There's more than one way of killing a cat.' I wasn't surprised, the idea had already penetrated that they could take care of themselves.

Certainly they could. They were occupying a room beyond the one they had broken into, which was a sort of scullery-outhouse, and they had made a bedsitter of what must have been the kitchen, a big vaulted place with built-in dresser and a range that would have cooked a horse. They had found three broken-down armchairs and stuffed the holes with newspaper.

'Two are Lalla's, the other's mine,' Gerda said. 'I don't need to stretch in bed.' They had the original kitchen table which was so heavy that no-one could have shifted it, a tea-chest for wardrobe and packs of paper cups, plates and air-line cutlery still in polythene wrappers. Lalla opened the door of the range on a clear, hot, liquid fire. 'Plenty of coke in the cellar,' said Gerda.

They told me to come again if I liked. I didn't know if I would like until Lalla took me out into the scullery and stood close.

'How do you manage?' I said. 'Heaving her about?'

'She can creep a bit.'

I went back the next day. The weather had turned unseasonably warm, a thick gold sun and leaves drifting down off the trees. I was on my motorbike, I knew the leaves would be falling in dead quiet and it struck me as sinister. Then I realised it wasn't the leaves and I nearly rode past Charlesworth. I wish I had, I wish to God I'd heeded the warning.

I turned into the drive, switched off the engine and walked the rest of the way. Somehow I didn't want to advertise myself, I suppose it was a bit of a defensive measure.

They were sitting outside taking the air, like a lot of people that last fine Sunday afternoon of the year. Gerda was in the armchair which also served as her bed, the castors had cut up the moss on the brick path when Lalla dragged it out. Gerda seemed to be asleep. Lalla was on her back on the grass, hands under her head, knees cocked and swaying to and fro, sort of lazily beckoning. She was a shape to dream of, I'd had many a dream about that girl before I ever saw her.

I propped the bike against a tree and crossed the grass. She had her eyes closed, she was smiling, lips parted to show the tip of her tongue. But for the old woman, one of my dreams would have come true then and there.

Gerda wasn't asleep. She says she never sleeps and I believe her. She may shut her eyes but she's watching, I swear I've seen the glitter of her eyes through her eyelids. 'What's that?' She pointed to my bike.

'A Yamaha Tri.'

'A motorbike? Can't you do any better?'

'It's not so bad.'

'It's no good to me.' I couldn't dispute that, nor could I see why I should. 'I need four wheels,' she said.

'A try-what?' said Lalla.

Her swaying knees mesmerised me. 'It's Japanese. 981 cc's, cush drive.'

'Why haven't you got a car?' Gerda's tongue came out too. I looked away.

'I can't afford to run one.'

'You know about cars? How to make them go?'

'Sure. You switch on the ignition and release the hand-brake.' It was my idea of a joke.

'Show him,' Gerda said. Lalla lay there, moving her knees. Gerda didn't raise her voice, she hurled it. 'Take him! Show him!'

'Take me,' I said to Lalla.

She raised herself slowly. When she stood upright her eyes blinked open like the eyes of a china doll.

'And me,' said Gerda, grinning.

Lalla smiled at my expression. 'Push the chair, it's easy.'

It wasn't. I was soon sweating, alternately

shoving and dragging the armchair with Gerda in it, I thought any moment it would fall apart, Lalla led the way round the house, across a yard to some outbuildings which had probably been stables. When she dragged open one of a pair of double doors the roof tiles heaved like rats under a blanket.

'Inside,' said Gerda, 'get me inside.' I managed to push the chair over the threshold, nearly tipping her out in the process. I couldn't see much except the shape of something big against the back wall. 'Go on,' she said, 'it won't bite you.'

It was dark in there and smelled of winter, all the winters, no summers. Then Lalla stepped inside and either it was my fancy or she really did light up the place. I saw that the something big was a car. I went to it through drifts of dead leaves and broken tiles.

'Well,' I said, 'well, well.'

It was a Studebaker convertible, thirty to forty years old, cased like a tank, bullet-nosed, with an aeroplane mascot and chrome wing strips. It was cobwebbed all over, loaded with dust, the wheel rims squatting on puddings of rotting rubber, the hood reduced to canvas rags stuck to a rusty frame. I've seldom seen such a heap, even in the breaker's yard.

'Can you make it go?' said Gerda. I laughed, I still thought her capable of a joke. Lalla climbed on the bonnet among the bird-droppings and posed like the girls do at the motor-show. I fooled around, whipped open the driver's door. The car gave a groan and settled deeper into its rust. 'Make it go,' said Gerda.

Half a crazy old woman without a claim in the world on me, gave a totally ridiculous order and suddenly I was dead scared. 'Look,' I said, 'do you take me for a fool?

Or a magician? This rubbish won't go in a million years.'

Gerda looked at me, not like a woman, even a crazy old one, more like a snake. All she said was, 'I can't wait that long,' and froze my blood.

I marched away down the drive to where I'd left my bike; if I knew what was good for me I wasn't coming here again. I sat in the saddle, my foot on the kick-start, then Lalla caught up with me. 'Do it to please me,' she said.

'You!'

'You could come whenever you fancied.'

'I wouldn't fancy.'

'No?' She pressed against me. 'Guess what it's like, alone with her, nothing to do, no telly, not even a radio. You could come in the evenings, we'd see each other as often as you like.'

'We can do that anyway.'

'In private, in there with the car.'

'What's she to you? Are you related?'

'God, no.'

'So why stay with her?'

Lalla has a way of buttoning her lip, childlike but not childish. 'That's my business.'

She was welcome to it. I wasn't drawn to her because of her beautiful nature and I didn't assume, as someone else might, that she stayed out of pity. I knew that she didn't stay as an act of charity or for any other reason. It was Gerda who kept her. And in my blood or my brains I sensed that I was in danger of being kept too. But Lalla drew me like a magnet. I took the risk, cocksure that I could handle it. And Lalla. I didn't begin to see that the dice was loaded.

I started going to Charlesworth in the evenings and working, pretending to, on the car. The first thing I did was clear out the back, and for a while everything went according to my plan. Lalla came to the garage and we had some very rewarding moments and knocked a lot of stuffing out of the back seat. The springs were still springy, the weather was mild, we weren't disturbed, and everything was laid on. Lalla was wonderful, the girl I'd always dreamed of having. I couldn't get enough of her. That, too, was laid on.

Then one evening she came late. I'd almost given up. Gerda, she said, was asking questions about what I was doing.

'Tell her we've been testing the rear axle,' I said.

Lalla didn't smile. 'Think she doesn't know?'

The next evening she didn't come at all. I waited, walked around the car, kicking it. For something to do, I tried to open the bonnet. The grips were rusted solid, I battered them free. Then I fetched the storm lantern which was all the lighting there was, and looked inside.

That engine wasn't a challenge so much as a black comedy. The battery had split and leaked. Only the fact that the car was built like a steamroller had stopped the acid eating through the wheel arch. Every bit of rubber was shrivelled, the wiring was scrambled, there was a bird's nest on the sump.

I started picking out the rubbish, dead leaves, beetle-cases, straws, and the next thing I knew I'd taken a rag and was cleaning off the rust. Next thing – you've guessed – I had started tinkering. But you won't guess how soon I forgot about Lalla. I worked, really worked, stripping that engine, until nearly midnight. When I say stripping, I mean simply stripping off the muck and frass of years. The next night I took solvents and white spirit and wire wool and a bundle of rags along with me. Just in case she doesn't come, I said to myself, I'll have something to do.

She did come. We got into the back of the car and I said, 'What happened to you yesterday?' Gerda had stopped her coming, she said. I nodded. 'Tied you to the kitchen table, did she? Or just knocked you out?'

Lalla said bitterly, 'Don't be so bloody naive.'

I was annoyed and didn't give her a chance to say more. She left soon after, without another word. I hung up the storm lantern and started chipping out the remains of the battery.

I spent three evenings cleaning up the engine and I promise you I was never so hard to please. When I work on the bike I'm not fussy. I'll check the parts are back in place, the screws tight, maybe I'll wipe off excess oil and grease, and that's it. Believe it or not, I chipped, scraped, rubbed and worked on that old wreck, scrupulous as if I was cutting and polishing a diamond. I kept stopping myself to ask why. Who I was doing it for? I had the answer, I couldn't believe that either.

She came one night when I was on my back sounding the chassis with a spanner. I didn't hear her, just felt the prickle up my spine as if something crawly had got into my shirt. I looked out from under the car and there she was, in the box-cart, her beak nose aimed at me. I said, 'How did you get here?'

She showed me how she propelled herself by pulling on the wheels of the pram frame. What she lacked in strength she made up for determination. Doubled over in her box, head down, arms flailing, she was like something trapped under a bowl. 'Where's Lalla?' I said.

'Gone into town for fish and chips. To celebrate.'

'Celebrate what?'

'The car's ready, isn't it?'

'Ready for the crusher, yes.'

She nodded, she seemed pleased. 'I can't afford to pay you, but you can come to supper.'

I said, 'I may as well tell you, this thing will never go on the road again.'

'Tomorrow you can take me for a drive.'

'Not on your life.'

'On my life,' she said, and her face shone with a sort of Day-glo light.

I said, 'I can understand you wanting to get out for a change of scene, but if it means so much to you, you could hire a car. Because even if this heap could be persuaded to move, you'd be risking your neck in it.'

She grinned, showing big yellow teeth. 'The last time I risked my neck I lost my legs. I jumped in front of a train, I was desperate. Wouldn't you be, after five hundred years?'

'What?'

'Nice legs I had. I miss them. They're dead and buried, like all my best bits. You should have seen me when I was young and whole, at Cumnor. You wouldn't have had eyes for Lalla. Or Amy.'

'Who?'

'Amy – Amy Robsart.' She was at the age when the face suddenly gapes open and you see how it's going to look when only the bones are left. 'Don't worry about my neck, no one can take that. Or my life.'

'I won't be responsible.'

'Someone has to be. You or Lalla. I don't care which. Dying's a private privilege, you might think, but not for me. I've got to take a young one with me. That's the law.'

'Law?'

'*Lex talionis.*'

I said, 'I don't know what you're talking about. What I'm saying is that it would cost a packet to put this ruin on the road. It's over forty years old, it's American and it's rusted into the ground. It would have to have tyres, battery, brake-linings, cylinders, piston-rods, valves – just about everything needs replacing. It would be cheaper to hire a chauffeur-driven Rolls for a month.'

'I want to ride in this car.'

'I don't.'

She propelled her box-cart forward and hit the Studebaker with her fist. 'One last ride and then comes the snapping of the traces, the end of the gay and empty journey.'

I was out of my depth and the last thing I wanted was to get into hers. 'I'll go pick Lalla up,' I said.

I met her coming along the lane with a parcel of fish and chips. As she climbed on the pillion behind me I told her, 'Gerda's mad. You ought to get away from her.'

'I'll never get away.'

'You can go any time you like.'

'No.'

'Why not?' She was holding me tight round my waist, I could smell the fish and chips and feel the warmth of it pressing into the small of my back. 'Anyway,' I said, 'she's old, she won't live for ever.'

'No?'

'Look,' I said, 'there are these couple of things everyone has to do – get born and die.'

'Do you know how old she is?'

'Eighty, ninety.'

'She's four hundred and thirty-two years old.'

I twisted round in the saddle. It was too dark to see Lalla's face. 'Great leg-pullers you two. I suppose that's how she lost hers.'

'She can't die.' Lalla's whisper tickled my ear. 'She did something hundreds of years ago, murdered someone, she won't say who, as a punishment she's condemned to keep on living. Unless—'

'Unless she doesn't,' I said, and blipped the throttle so as not to hear any more nonsense.

Lalla shouted, 'You've heard of the Flying Dutchman!'

'That old film with Ava Gardner?'

'Film? God, you're crude.'

I won't say I finished work on the car, because I didn't do half what I should. I salvaged four tyres and a battery from the breaker, a friend found me some plugs. I reckoned if the thing didn't move it wouldn't want brakes, but I put in oil and petrol. The radiator pissed like a baby when I filled it. Never mind, I thought, it can't boil dry.

Every day Gerda asked was the car ready. When I told her yes, she stuck out her tongue, it might have been for glee but she looked like a lizard catching flies. 'Tomorrow we'll go for a ride,' she said.

The next day was a Sunday. I had a few drinks at the pub to set me up, then rode out to Charlesworth.

Gerda was ready and waiting in the back of the banger. Seeing her sitting there like gentry, bolt upright, her woolly hat on her head, I remembered what she'd said about being related to an earl. She scared me most when I thought she might be speaking the truth.

'Where's Lalla?' I said.

'Why do you always want to know where Lalla is? We don't need her. Drive away!'

'Not without Lalla.'

I kicked the front tyre which was bald as a coot. Gerda gave me a look which would have killed if she hadn't needed me alive. She banged on the side of the car. Lalla came out of the shadows and slipped into the front seat without a word or look in my direction.

'I can't take this on the road, it's not taxed or insured.'

'I don't care,' said Gerda.

'I do. It could put me in jail.'

'You needn't go on the road,' said Lalla, 'there's a cart-track that joins with the drive and goes for miles.'

Now I hadn't even attempted to start the engine, not out of curiosity or anything else. I had no curiosity about the wreck, it was just something I was lumbered with and struggling to get shot of. I sat behind the wheel thinking that with any luck the wheel would come away in my hands. I thought the ignition won't work, it can't, there's no circuit. 'Here goes,' I said. I sounded like my father when he used to play with me on the kitchen floor when I was small. I pulled out the choke, turned the ignition key and flattened the accelerator pedal to the floorboards.

If you know anything about motors, you're not going to believe this. There was an explosion and a sort of scream as if a rocket had been fired. That paralytic old engine started first go.

Panicking, I rammed in bottom gear and we moved with a noise like an iron foundry. Tiles, shocked off the roof, crashed all round us. We lumbered across the yard, I just managed to clear the wall of the house and we were on the drive.

If you know anything about motors you'll appreciate that the steering was diabolical. I needed to brace myself, feet on the floorboards, to hold the wheel – and I wanted my feet to operate the pedals. As soon as I dared, I changed up. The gears shrieked: something – power or fury or blue murder – belted through the chassis. The dead weight of rusty metal surged forward, we were away, breaking through undergrowth, wallowing in and out of potholes, crushing fallen branches, careering over boulders, roaring and smoking. Like a rogue elephant. And about as tractable. I stamped the brake pedal down to the floor. Nothing happened. I pulled on the handbrake. There was a noise like tearing lino and a smell like a tar-boiler. The car shied slightly and kept on going.

I spend a lot of time now trying not to think about certain things: I try not to think about that ride. It took twenty years off my life, burned them off in minutes. I'll never be young again.

My only consolation, though I had no chance to savour it, was the fact that we weren't on the public highway. If other people's lives weren't at risk, ours were. I clung to that wheel, bracing my legs till they were ready to break, fighting to engage a lower gear and slow us down. I was sweating the slimy sweat of fear, my body slipped about under my clothes, as potent as a wet paper bag.

'Can't you go any faster?' Gerda was beating the back of my seat, in another minute I thought she'd beat me, ride me like a jockey. Her face in the mirror had that grinning glare.

'Can't you drive?' said Lalla. She too was smiling.

They had perfect confidence in me or they simply didn't care. Either way I was on my own.

The driveway had become a rutted track running through beechwoods. The trees, stripped for winter, had put iron-hard roots across the track. Every time we hit them at speed I expected we'd overturn, and burst into flames. I already saw the fire, heard my own screams. Suddenly I knew why Gerda reminded me of guy fawkes. She was programmed to burn, and me with her.

The track, which had been level, started to descend. The car picked up speed under its own weight. It seemed to exult. We swooped into blackness. I thought we were running through a railway tunnel. The headlamps, of course, didn't work. I prayed, 'Holy Mary, Mother of God—' I'm not Catholic, it just seemed more hopeful to appeal to a woman.

'It's like the Tunnel of Love!' cried Lalla.

'Faster, faster!' shouted Gerda.

Then we were out into space, and light which was more than daylight. Even in the state I was in I knew it for the cold flat light off the sea. The awful din, the grinding and groaning of the chassis, the clattering of the doors and mudguards and bonnet flaps, subsided a little, we were running across downland turf. But the engine was working itself to a frenzy. I prayed to Christ – a man might be better able to understand our situation – that it would blow up. I knew where we were – on Pendarrow Head. It's a narrow spur of cliff and we were belting across it to the sea.

I pumped at the brakes. The pedal snapped under my foot. I tried to get into lower gear and got into neutral. Sick with horror, I felt that bloody car leap forward like a greyhound out of the trap. Straight for a one-hundred foot drop to the rocks.

I didn't see Lalla get out. The next I knew, the offside door was batting to and fro on its hinges and the passenger seat was empty. I wrenched the steering-wheel from side to side to try to slow us. I wasn't reasoning straight, but I hoped if we turned turtle we just might stop rolling before we got to the edge.

That car wasn't going to slow and it certainly wasn't going to stop. If I wanted to live, I knew I had to get out. Fast. I let go of the wheel, ready to throw myself over the side. But I couldn't. I couldn't move. Gerda had me by the shoulders, she gripped me from behind with a strength I would never have credited her with. She was shouting in my ear, 'Faster, faster!' Maybe it was, 'Bastard, bastard!'

We came off Pendarrow Head at sixty miles an hour, me wondering how I'd die, feet up, or head down. It couldn't be too quick, it couldn't be quick enough.

As a matter of fact, I'm still waiting. We hit the water in a belly-flop, I remember seeing walls of water standing up all round me. Then came blackness, and roaring in my head, and the cold that kills. Death is every-where at once – I found that out. Something was taking me down, and it wasn't only the weight of the car. I know now that it was Gerda. She had her hands on my shoulders, forcing me to go with her to the bottom of the sea.

True, the dice were loaded against me, but I have a life expectancy and I didn't mean to lose it to Gerda. I went berserk down there on the sea-bed, I bet they'd never seen any-thing like it before. I literally smashed my way out of the car, I broke off the steering-wheel and kicked in the dash.

But I couldn't get away from Gerda. Her fingers dug into my bones. I carry the marks of her nails to this day. It was the car that saved me. The bottom fell out, I was sucked down, torn out of Gerda's grip by the weight of the engine.

They say you surface three times before you die of drowning. The hell you do. I came up just the once, and if I'd gone down once again it would have finished me. When I got the air in my lungs I drank it, swallowed it, scoffed it wholesale. Then I struck out with arms, legs, everything I had.

What I had was mostly panic. I was scared of drowning and scared rigid of drowning with Gerda. I knew that she was somewhere underneath and it wasn't the sea clawing me back, it was her.

The tide was in. It rolled me to and fro like a lump of bladderwrack, for anyone watching it must have been a laugh a minute. Somehow I got a footing on a knife-edge of rock. Next minute it sheared into my chest as I was flung down. But I held to it for dear life, and when the waves screeched back over the shingle I got my knees where my hands were. While the next waves swamped over me, I clung on, when they receded I crawled over the rocks to the beach.

There wasn't time to rest. The sea was licking at the base of the cliff. In the high days of summer, picnic parties, kids with buckets and spades, Lilos and rubber dinghies, frequent this beach. A path has been cut into the cliff for their convenience. And mercifully for me.

I scrambled up it. I wouldn't want a dog to feel like I did then, soaked to the bone, sea – or tears – leaking from every pore. My breathing deafened me. I dragged myself up over the cliff and fell on my face.

I could have died there, I wouldn't have minded dying on my own. The bitter wind sweeping across the headland, and something else – a feeling that I was watched, got me to my elbows. I propped myself on my arms and looked around.

Lalla was reclining on the grass a few feet away. 'You might have killed her,' she said.

I managed to croak, 'What about me?'

'It was what she hoped.' Lalla was eyeing me with distaste. 'God, you're a mess.'

I said, 'I nearly drowned, I'm half dead, and she's all dead—'

'Fat chance.'

'What?'

Lalla pointed out to sea.

I'll be able to see what I saw then till the day I die, whether my eyes are open or shut. I see it now. The old car was floating – yes, floating right way up – just beyond the rocks. In the back sat Gerda. She took off her woolly hat and waved it.

'Mother of God!' – who else could I say it to? – 'She's not drowned!'

'Of course not,' said Lalla. 'You didn't stay with her.'

'Stay with her!'

'You were meant to. She was all set to die, but she can't unless she takes someone with her.' It wasn't distaste Lalla was eyeing me with, it was dislike. 'Someone young, lover-boy.'